Tom & Tony Bradman

Illustrated by Si Clark

A & C Black • London

For Joe, rebalancing the odds.

First published 2011 by
A & C Black Publishers Ltd
36 Soho Square, London, W1D 3QY

www.acblack.com

ISBN 978-1-4081-2376-8

A CIP catalogue for this book is available from the British Library.

Printed and bound in Great Britain
by CPI Cox & Wyman, Reading, RG1 8EX.

'There is absolutely no *way* you're going to beat me next time, Luke Riley,' snarled Yasmin, her eyes narrowed as she stared at him across the table. 'Not unless you cheat, of course. But then I wouldn't put that past you, either.'

'I don't need to cheat, Yasmin,' Luke said, shrugging and smiling at her. 'And even if I did, you'd never know. I'd be the best cheat in the galaxy.'

'Huh, there's a fine line between being confident and being a big-head,' muttered Yuri. 'Mind you, I'm not surprised you keep winning, Luke. It's not easy to concentrate in here. I can hardly think straight with all this noise.'

Luke winced as something landed with a *CRASH!* on the deck behind him. He looked up from his computer at the total chaos around them. Clarke, their teacher, had slipped out for a moment to talk to the teacher in the classroom next door. And of course, the instant he'd gone, the kids of Primary One had stopped doing the work he had set them and had started having fun instead.

For Luke and his two friends, that had meant playing computer games. Yuri had quickly plugged his trusty laptop into their table's data input socket. Then he had networked their terminals so they could compete with each other in a classic flight simulator called War Beyond the Stars. But just about everyone else seemed to think their freedom was a perfect opportunity to misbehave.

Some kids were playing wild games of chase, two boys were play-fighting and had knocked over a chair (hence the *CRASH!*), and a girl was pretending to be their teacher at his desk and making her friends scream with laughter.

'Well, the noise doesn't bother me,' said Luke, turning back to his friends, brown-skinned Yasmin with her jet-black hair in a neat ponytail, and the flame-haired, freckle-faced Yuri. 'So I'm up for another game...if you are, that is.'

'Hah, you bet!' said Yasmin. 'Come on, Yuri. Let's thrash this big-head!'

'You'll be lucky,' laughed Luke, and soon they were deeply immersed in the game. Each player was the pilot of a super-cool combat craft armed with laser cannons and space torpedoes, the goal being to get through your opponent's defences and destroy their base. Yuri and Yasmin worked together and made things pretty difficult for Luke – but he was still sure he could beat them.

After all, he had spent a lot of time playing computer games since they'd left

Earth. There wasn't much else to do on the spaceship *Buzz Aldrin*, with its small cargo of humanity searching for a new home somewhere among the stars. Luke often thought that if it weren't for computer games and having a couple of great friends like Yuri and Yasmin he would have gone barmy a long time ago.

'Hey, that's not fair!' squealed Yasmin suddenly. 'I told you he'd cheat!'

'Yeah, Luke, you're only supposed to have one combat craft, not hundreds!' groaned Yuri. 'How did you manage to create a whole fleet for yourself?'

Luke stopped tapping at his keyboard and peered at his screen, where a swarm of small spaceships had appeared. He'd never seen anything quite like them in any game he'd played. They were strange and spiky and menacing.

'But I didn't!' said Luke. 'They've got nothing to do with me, I swear!'

Just then the classroom door hissed open and Luke glanced up, expecting to see Clarke – but it was Captain Riley, commander of the *Buzz Aldrin*. She was also Luke's mum, and he could see she wasn't happy. She scanned the chaos with a look on her face that could have frozen an exploding super-nova.

'*QUIET!*' she yelled. 'I was heading to the bridge and I could hear the racket you're making three corridors away! What is going on? And where in space is your teacher? Stop misbehaving and get back to your seats *immediately*!'

'Whoa, your mum is one scary lady,' said Yasmin, admiration in her voice. 'I bet she could get *anybody* to stop what they're doing and behave themselves.'

'You got that right,' said Luke. 'So we don't want her to catch us playing games in class when we should be working. Er... over to you, Yuri.'

'I'm already on it, Luke,' said Yuri. Within a few seconds War Beyond the Stars had been replaced on their screens by the

work they should have been doing. The class had quickly settled down too. All the other children were now back at their tables, concentrating on their screens and trying to look like little angels.

'That's better,' said Captain Riley, taking down her glare a notch. She came over and stood beside Luke's table. 'And what were you three rogues up to? You were suspiciously quiet – I can't believe you were actually working.'

'Hey, that's so unfair!' said Luke, putting on his best expression of outraged innocence. 'I think you'd be pretty surprised at just how hard we can work!'

Little did he know they were all in for a very big surprise indeed.

CHAPTER TWO
CLOSE ENCOUNTER

The door hissed open again and Clarke hurried in. He was a hologram, but he looked human. To be more precise, he was the spitting image of Albert Einstein, right down to his shock of white hair and his droopy moustache.

'Oh, good morning, Captain Riley!' he murmured, frowning. 'Er... I wasn't expecting to see you here. I do hope the children were behaving themselves.'

Captain Riley opened her mouth to reply, but she didn't get the chance. A *BLEEP! BLEEP!* noise came from the communicator screen on the wall.

'Bridge calling Captain Riley!' said a voice Luke recognised. It belonged to Lieutenant Chung, one of the ship's officers. Mum walked over and touched the screen and Chung's face appeared, her eyes worried beneath her dark fringe.

'What can I do for you, Lieutenant?' said Mum. 'Do we have a problem?'

'I'm not sure, Captain,' said Chung. 'But I think you should see this.'

The picture on the screen changed to show the deep blackness of space. A large star was shining in the far distance with a trio of dark, shadowy planets circling it. Luke's gaze, however, was drawn to something else – a swarm of strange, spiky – and familiar – spaceships heading towards the *Buzz Aldrin*.

'I don't believe it!' whispered Yasmin. 'We saw those ships in the game!'

'Yeah, we did,' murmured Luke. 'I don't get how that can happen.'

'Beats me too,' said Yuri, tapping at his laptop. 'Interesting, though...'

'We've tried communicating with them, Captain, but they haven't responded to us yet,' Chung was saying. 'And we just can't scan them, either. They seem to have the same kind of force field round them as two of the planets.'

Unlike the rest of the class, Luke knew what Chung was talking about because Mum had told him at dinner the night before – being the captain's son did have advantages. They had arrived in this star system a few days previously and had immediately begun to survey all three planets. One was a barren rock, but they hadn't been able to find out anything about the other two. Both were surrounded by force fields the *Buzz Aldrin*'s scanners couldn't penetrate.

'I can see that they're on an interception course with us,' said Mum, scowling at the screen, her arms folded. 'What kind of speed are they doing?'

'They're moving pretty fast,' said Chung, tapping at the panel again. 'At this rate we could be having a close encounter with them in the next few minutes.'

'Right, I'm on my way to the bridge,' Mum said grimly, turning to leave.

'Oh dear, that all sounds rather serious, Captain,' said Clarke. 'I hope they turn out to be nice, whoever they are. Er... is there anything I should do?'

Luke suddenly realised that Clarke and everyone else in the classroom had been listening intently to the conversation between Mum and Chung too. Clarke looked anxious, and most of the children were wide-eyed with worry as well.

'Not really,' snapped Mum. 'Apart from staying with your class and keeping them under control, that is. Now if you'll excuse me, I have to be elsewhere.'

'I'm terribly sorry, Captain,' Clarke spluttered. 'I didn't realise they'd – '

'Hang on, Captain,' Chung said. 'One of the ships has broken away from the rest. It's moving incredibly quickly – and heading for us on a collision course!'

'*What?!*' said Mum, turning back to her. 'How long have we got?'

'Seconds at the most!' Chung yelled. 'Too late for evasive action...'

'Go to red alert, Chung!' said Mum, glancing over her shoulder at Luke. He nodded to her, then looked at Yuri and Yasmin, and they moved closer together. Yuri unplugged his precious laptop and held it against his chest to protect it.

'Aye aye, Captain!' Chung replied, and Luke saw her hit a big red button on the panel in front of her. A *WHOOP-WHOOP* sound instantly filled the ship, red lights on the ceiling started flashing, and some of the children screamed.

'WARNING! WARNING!' intoned a computerised voice. 'COLLISION IMPACT IN TEN SECONDS AND COUNTING. NINE, EIGHT...'

'Brace yourselves, everybody!' yelled Mum. 'Hang on to something!'

'Er... I'd just like to say it's been good knowing you two,' said Luke.

'Oh, stop it,' said Yasmin, and rolled her

eyes. 'We're not dead yet.'

'Ah, but we might be soon,' Yuri said brightly. 'A collision at the kind of speed that ship is going will do a lot of damage to the *Buzz*...'

'*JUST SHUT UP, YURI!*' Yasmin and Luke yelled at their geeky friend.

'THREE... TWO... ONE...' intoned the computer. 'IMPACT!' And then there was a terrific CLANG! of metal hitting metal, the two hulls crashing together. Luke felt the deck judder beneath his feet – and watched horrified as a white dot appeared on the wall beside him and quickly became a fizzing, smoking line.

Someone was cutting right through the ship's hull – from the outside.

18

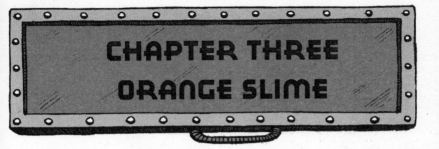

CHAPTER THREE
ORANGE SLIME

The white dot quickly traced a curve in the hull, cutting a ragged circle two metres across, molten metal dribbling down the bulkhead. Luke was hypnotised and couldn't tear his eyes away, although behind him he could hear Mum yelling at the children to get out. Everything seemed to have gone into slow motion too. Yuri and Yasmin just managed to drag him back as a huge slab of hull-plating fell inwards and crushed their table with a mighty *CLANG!*

There was a brief silence, and Luke wondered why they hadn't been sucked into the vacuum of space. Then suddenly several creatures that looked like giant insects skittered out of the hole in the hull. They had huge heads with antennae, enormous bug eyes and clacking jaws, long, narrow bodies made of some dark red, shiny shell-like substance, and lots of thin,

spidery limbs. And each one was holding a serious-looking weapon too, some kind of laser rifle.

There was a sharp intake of breath from nearly everyone in the classroom – and then most of the kids screamed, including Luke, Yasmin and Yuri.

'Run, Luke!' yelled Mum. But it was too late. One of the alien bugs opened its mouth wide and spat out a stream of sticky orange slime that covered the three friends. Luke tried to shake it off, but the ooze hardened and he found himself trapped in a rigid cocoon. Luckily his eyes weren't covered so he could still see what was happening. The giant bugs grabbed the cocooned forms of Yuri and Yasmin and threw them out of the hole, and did the same to Luke.

He travelled a short distance and hit

some kind of wall that yielded slightly, then fell onto a floor with a loud *SQUELCH!* He realised he was in the alien spaceship which had been on a collision course with the *Buzz Aldrin* – it must have somehow locked onto their hull. He looked round, but there was no sign of Yasmin and Yuri. The hole they had come through was beginning to close as well, at least on this side. Then he felt another hole opening beneath him...

Luke screamed as he was sucked head-first into a dark, slimy tube that held him tight and pulsed like some living thing, pushing him downwards. He closed his eyes, convinced he was about to be digested in the stomach of some colossal alien creature – but seconds later he shot out of the tube and landed on the floor of another chamber with a *THUD!* that drove the breath clean out of his lungs.

'Are you OK, Luke?' said a familiar voice, and Yasmin's face appeared above his. She had slime on her hair and cheeks, but she seemed able to move.

'I think so,' said Luke, trying to sit up and succeeding. His own cocoon was softening, most of the slime falling off him. 'What about you and Yuri?'

'I'm fine, although I don't think my hair will ever be the same again,' said Yasmin, scowling. 'And Yuri couldn't be happier. He's in geek heaven.'

Luke stood up and saw that Yuri was studying their surroundings, his precious laptop tucked under one arm. 'Fascinating...' Yuri murmured. They were in a circular chamber seemingly made of the same shell-like substance as the aliens themselves. But part of the wall was transparent, and through it Luke could see the *Buzz Aldrin* growing smaller as the ship they were in flew away.

'Do you think they're OK with the hull breached like that?' said Luke.

'Probably,' said Yuri, coming over to stand beside Luke. 'The emergency force fields are designed to seal a breach like that almost immediately.'

'*Almost* immediately?' squeaked Luke. 'But what if they were too late?'

Yuri shook his head and sighed at Luke's sad lack of knowledge. Then he started explaining the *Buzz Aldrin*'s emergency force field system in detail.

'Could we talk about something else, guys?' Yasmin said crossly. 'Like what is happening, and, I don't know, maybe how we could save ourselves?'

'We've been kidnapped,' said Luke, shrugging. 'I've got no idea why.'

'If you ask me, we'll find out down there,' said Yuri, nodding at the large planet that was just coming into view. 'At this speed we'll be there soon.'

But they were about to arrive on the planet even more quickly than Yuri thought. Suddenly the floor softened and swallowed them. They screamed, fearing the worst, but found themselves in a cramped, transparent bubble which was immediately fired out of the spaceship. It zoomed past the alien fleet then hurtled towards the planet, fizzing and sparking briefly as it shot through what seemed to be a gigantic energy field, all crackling lines of light and power.

The planet's surface loomed in front of them. Luke gaped at vast oceans and steaming jungles, and a huge column like an enormous termite nest dead ahead.

'Oh wow,' murmured Yuri, his eyes wide. 'Look at that – it's *fantastic.*'

'Not to me, it isn't,' said Yasmin. 'If there's one thing I hate, it's bugs.'

Luke didn't say anything. He wasn't too keen on them himself.

CHAPTER FOUR
SPECIAL MISSION

It soon became obvious their destination was the huge column. The bubble eventually came to a halt and hovered directly over the great tower of rock, the three friends peering nervously into the hollow interior below them. But they could see only a few metres down – below was utter darkness.

'So what happens now?' muttered Yasmin, scowling as she pulled orange gunge out of her hair. 'I hope they don't keep us hanging around like this.'

'Er... I don't think they're going to,' murmured Luke, an edge of panic in his voice. He and Yuri were staring into the giant column with their eyes wide.

'What are you talking about?' said Yasmin, following their gaze. Then her eyes grew wide too, and her mouth fell open. 'I don't believe I'm seeing that.'

An incredibly long pink tendril was snaking up and out of the column. It rose above them and seized the bubble, curling round it like a frog's tongue lazily catching a fly in mid-air. Then the tendril whipped back, and the children screamed as they were plunged into darkness and rapidly pulled down the column's entire length. Luke felt sick and closed his eyes tight, convinced they were about to be swallowed for real this time... but that didn't happen.

Suddenly he felt the bubble being dropped. It rolled across a bumpy surface, the three friends tumbling over each other like rag dolls in a washing machine. They came to rest at last, and Luke dared to open his eyes just in time to see the bubble begin to soften, then vanish with a soft *PLOP!* The three friends were left sprawled on the floor of a colossal chamber, its roof fifty metres above, its walls full of large, shadowy holes. The only light was an eerie green glow that came from some kind of alien moss growing in patches on the rock.

But even in the poor light Luke could see they weren't alone. The whole chamber was full of giant alien insects like the ones that had grabbed them on the *Buzz Aldrin*. They scuttled in and out of the holes and scurried across the floor of the chamber, all of them making strange clicking and buzzing noises.

'Welcome to Bug Central,' muttered Yasmin. 'What a nightmare!'

'Huh, you can say that again,' whispered

Luke, getting to his feet. 'Well, what do we do now? Any suggestions, you guys?'

'We should try to communicate, of course!' said Yuri. 'You know, tell them we're peaceful explorers and we want to be their friends, that sort of thing.'

'Oh yeah?' said Yasmin. 'I had a different kind of communication in mind. I'd like to find whoever's in charge down here and give him such a hard time!'

'I think you're about to get your chance,' said Luke. 'Check out the big bug.'

A large alien had emerged from a hole on the far side of the chamber and was scuttling towards them. Another half dozen aliens were close behind, all armed with laser rifles like the bugs that had burst onto the *Buzz Aldrin*. The large alien stopped at last in front of the children, and now Luke could see he was wearing a tight, shiny uniform covered in small pieces of metal, like medals. The alien looked uncomfortable, his body bulging out of the uniform in several places.

'I bid you welcome,' the alien said in a squeaky voice. 'I am Prime Admiral K'Klem-Tek, leader of the mightiest race in the universe...the P'tush-faar!'

'WE ARE THE P'TUSH-FAAR!' the bugs

behind him squeaked loudly. Then they clicked and buzzed like mad and waved their laser rifles over their heads.

'Never heard of you,' said Yasmin. The clicking and buzzing grew louder, but Yasmin stood her ground. 'And I'd like to know why you think it's OK to attack our spaceship and bring us down here to this nest, or whatever it is.'

'Ah... I regret your presence, and that of the pale skinny one,' said the Prime Admiral. 'I gave strict orders that only The-Amazing-Super-Space-Combat-Pilot-Luke-Riley was to be taken, but my soldiers couldn't tell you apart.'

'*Amazing-Super-Space-Combat-Pilot-Luke-Riley*?' said Yasmin, laughing. 'Where in space did you get that? Luke isn't amazing or super or even a...'

'They probably got it from me,' Luke

murmured, blushing, a strange thought starting to take shape in his mind. 'It's how I sign myself in for War Beyond the Stars. I think they've somehow managed to hack into the *Buzz*'s computers.'

'Ah, Luke Riley!' said Admiral K'Klem-Tek, turning to him and clicking with excitement, the others doing the same. 'Your skills as a combat pilot are truly incredible! We have studied all your campaigns and brought you here to take on a great task, a special mission that can only end in death or glory!'

'DEATH OR GLORY!' squeaked the soldier bugs behind him, and soon hundreds more gathered round the children and joined in. 'DEATH OR GLORY, DEATH OR GLORY!' they chanted. 'LUKE RILEY, DEATH OR GLORY!'

Luke stood there in the sea of noise, wishing he could be anywhere else.

The aliens quietened down eventually, and Luke got the Admiral to do some more explaining. It turned out the P'Tush-faar had started scanning the *Buzz Aldrin* as soon as it had arrived in the star system. They had hacked into the ship's computer – and seen something that interested them.

'We saw immediately that the mighty Luke Riley was the one to help us defeat the C'Haaf-shaar and destroy them forever!' squeaked the Admiral.

Apparently the C'Haaf-shaar were a species of lizards that lived on the other planet the *Buzz Aldrin* hadn't been able to scan, and the P'Tush-faar had been at war with them for thousands of years. Nobody could remember why the war had started in the first place, although the admiral did have a lot of nasty things to say about the enemy, and called them some very unpleasant names.

Recently the P'Tush-faar had developed a mega-bomb to destroy the C'Haaf-shaar's planet. But both sides had long ago devised defences their pilots weren't skilful enough to penetrate. Then suddenly the *Buzz Aldrin* had appeared, and the P'Tush-faar believed they had found someone who could do the job for them – The-Amazing-Super-Space-Combat-Pilot-Luke-Riley.

'Oh, I get it now!' said Yasmin. 'You thought what you saw us doing was real and that Luke here is a brilliant pilot. I mean, just how dumb is that?'

'Actually, Yasmin, you're being a bit unfair – War Beyond the Stars is a particularly realistic game,' said Yuri. Then he smiled and turned to address the Admiral. 'And may I say that entering the game in disguise was a nice touch?'

'And may *I* say that you can be a real creep sometimes?' hissed Yasmin.

'Game?' said the Admiral with a flurry of confused clicking. 'What is a... game? I do not understand. This is something we have never heard of.'

'Huh, why am I not surprised by that?' said Yasmin with a snort. 'You'd better give him the bad news, Luke. Then we can get them to take us home.'

All eyes swivelled to stare at Luke expectantly now, alien and human. He cleared his throat, and wondered what he should say in such a tricky situation.

'Well... I'm sorry to be a disappointment, Admiral,' he said at last. 'I just don't think I'll be able to help you. I'm sure I could probably do the job, but...'

Yasmin snorted and rolled her eyes, and Luke stuck his tongue out at her.

'Of course you can!' said the Admiral. 'We have seen how you defeated many powerful enemies – the Ishtreen Alliance, the Zofari Entity, the Vark...'

'But none of those are *real*,' said Luke. The Admiral looked at him blankly, so Luke tried explaining to him what 'playing a game' meant, and Yuri and Yasmin joined in.

The Admiral listened, occasionally making clicking noises. Luke began to think that he was getting through to him. He stopped talking after a while and waited for the Admiral to speak. There was a long pause, almost as if the Admiral was processing it all in his brain.

'No, I'm afraid I still don't understand,' the Admiral said at last. 'Now, if you'd care to come with me I'll explain the attack plan to you in detail.'

'I don't believe it,' Luke groaned, exasperated. 'Listen, I'm going to make this really easy for you. I wouldn't do what you want me to even if I could. I won't help you destroy a whole planet! Your war's got nothing to do with me.'

'Yeah, you tell him, Luke!' said Yasmin. 'We don't blow up planets!'

'Well, that's not strictly true, Yasmin,' said Yuri with a stern look. 'If you remember, our adventure with Alpha ended in the destruction of a planet...'

'OK, then, fussy boots,' sighed Yasmin, rolling her eyes. 'We don't usually blow up planets *deliberately*, and we certainly don't get involved in wars.'

'So that's it, then,' said Luke, smiling at the Admiral. 'Sorry about the misunderstanding, but maybe next time you won't hack into the computers of complete strangers! And my advice would be to try and make friends with these lizards. Er... you should all just try to... get... along...'

Luke let his voice fade into silence. The Admiral was staring at him, and Luke could tell that his mood had changed. He looked cross in the way that only a giant alien bug-eyed monster in a tight-fitting uniform can.

'So, you refuse to fight for the P'Tush-faar in our hour of need?' he said. 'I'm afraid that is not acceptable. Either you do as we ask – or we kill you!'

The Admiral snapped out an order to the soldier bugs behind him, and the three friends found themselves staring down the silver barrels of half a dozen laser rifles. They looked at each other – and slowly raised their hands.

'Well, if you put it like that...' murmured Luke. 'Amazing-Super-Space-Combat-Pilot-Luke-Riley reporting for duty, Admiral!'

The situation seemed to be even trickier than he had thought.

CHAPTER SIX
HOSTILE FIGHTERS

Luke, Yasmin and Yuri were hustled along to another part of the nest. At first Luke felt nervous, wondering if they were going to be cocooned in orange slime again and grabbed by the giant pink tendril. But the aliens merely hurried them down long, dark, narrow tunnels, clicking and buzzing, the Admiral in the lead.

Eventually they came to another large chamber – and the three friends were amazed at what they saw. Standing in the centre of the chamber was a space-fighter – *Luke's* space-fighter. It looked exactly the same as the ship he always flew in the game. The same bullet-shaped central hull, the same tail-fins, the same weapons modules on either wing.

'That is so... *cool*,' he whispered.

'Except for that ugly great thing hanging under it,' said Yasmin.

Luke saw what Yasmin was talking about. An evil-looking cylinder made of black metal was attached to the underside of the fighter – the mega-bomb.

'As you can see, we've even built you a replica of your own ship,' said the Prime Admiral. The children were ushered up a ladder by the Admiral's guards and took their places in the cockpit. Luke sat in the pilot's seat, with Yuri and Yasmin in seats just behind him. The aliens left, and immediately the roof of the chamber began to open, a pair of massive doors slowly sliding apart.

The cockpit radio buzzed and the Admiral's voice came out of the speakers. 'I'm sending you the battle plan now,' he said. 'All you have to do is drop the mega-bomb anywhere on the planet's surface.'

Graphics showing the other planet appeared on one of the screens in front of Luke. It was surrounded by thousands of heavily armed satellites and

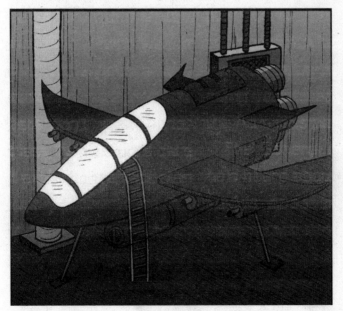

space-fighters. Every inch of space for hundreds of kilometres was covered by some kind of deadly weapon. 'Then we will be victorious! DEATH OR GLORY!' the Admiral chanted. 'DEATH OR – '

'Yeah, whatever,' muttered Luke, cutting him off with an electronic squawk. He was already studying the fighter's controls. They looked pretty simple – a joystick, firing buttons for weapons, tactical data scanners, sensors. Luke smiled. They were in an awful situation – but he couldn't help feeling that this part was a dream come true.

'Right, seat belts on, you two,' he said. 'Time to see whether they've built this thing properly.'

He fired up the engines and the fighter rose gently from the floor. Then he hit the main thrusters and they blasted off on a pillar of fire, the g-force pushing them back into their seats. Seconds later they were in space, shooting away from the planet of the P'Tush-faar and cruising along at speed. The aliens had built the fighter properly. It was incredibly fast and nippy, a real joy to fly.

'Hey, the scanners are showing the *Buzz*!' said Yuri. He had managed to plug his laptop into the fighter's computer. 'It looks OK, and it's not that far away.'

'What a relief!' said Yasmin. 'Come on, Luke – let's just make a run for it.'

'That could be tricky,' Luke said, nodding at the screen showing the fighter's reverse view. The whole P'Tush-faar fleet was very close behind them. 'They'll probably shoot us down if we try to escape, and they might even take out the *Buzz*, too. No, I think we ought to go along with it for the time being.

Once we get through the other aliens' defences we can tell them about the mega-bomb and ask them to protect us from this nasty lot. Then we can contact my mum.'

'That sounds far too complicated,' said Yasmin. 'And way too dangerous!'

'Watch out, Luke!' Yuri said suddenly. 'Hostile fighters heading for us.'

'I see them,' muttered Luke. A crowd of fighters from the other planet swept in towards them, firing their laser cannons, the glittering beams scorching past. Luke threw his fighter to one side, then the other, and soon he'd got through the first line of defence. But he soon realised that had just been the easy part.

'Seven, eight... no, *fourteen* enemy ships on our tail!' Yuri yelled. 'They're firing missiles!' Explosions blossomed around the fighter, but Luke kept going, dodging through fields of space mines, plunging through an energy field – and at last they saw the planet below, its dark, ominous bulk looming up at them.

Luke eased up on the speed and took the fighter in low, skimming across the brown, rocky surface, looking for a place to set the fighter down. He spotted a flat area near a cluster of dome-like structures, and seconds later they landed with a slight bump, their view through the cockpit obscured by a cloud of dust.

'Not bad, Riley,' said Yasmin. 'But I still think I'm a better pilot than you.'

'No way!' said Luke. 'I was *awesome*, even if I do say so myself.'

'Careful, now!' said Yasmin. 'If your head gets any bigger it might pop.'

'Er... guys?' said Yuri. 'Could you stop arguing? We've got company.'

Luke and Yasmin turned to look out of the cockpit. The dust had settled, and they were surrounded by hundreds of giant lizards pointing weapons at them.

They all seemed pretty angry.

CHAPTER SEVEN
HISSY FITS

When Luke had set off for school that morning, he had never thought he would end up meeting an alien leader, let alone two – and on separate planets, come to that. But oddly enough, even though they were from different species, Supreme General G'Gral-Harg and Prime Admiral K'Klem-Tek had a lot in common.

They both wore tight uniforms, the General's body bulging out of his, just like the Admiral's. They both had squeaky voices. And they were both rather dim.

'No, I don't understand,' the Supreme General said, and shook his giant lizard head. The C'Haaf-shaar were about the same size as the P'Tush-faar, but were scarier to look at. They bore a strong resemblance to an ancient Earth dinosaur species – T-Rex. 'I have never heard of this thing you call a *game*.'

Luke sighed. After they'd landed, he and Yasmin and Yuri had been dragged off to see the General in one of the dome-like structures. The General had sat there, surrounded by soldiers armed with lasers, listening as Luke had tried to explain about being kidnapped by the P'Tush-faar and the Admiral's plan.

The General had got very angry when he'd heard about the mega-bomb, and the soldiers had all had hissy fits too. Then they had said the same kind of unpleasant stuff about the P'Tush-faar as the Admiral had said about them.

'This isn't going very well, is it, guys?' Yasmin whispered. 'I think we should just give them the mega-bomb and high-tail it back to the *Buzz*.'

'I heard that!' squeaked the General. 'And it would not be acceptable! I have a much better idea. We will turn the P'Tush-faar's treachery on them. You, Luke Riley, will fly their own mega-bomb back to their planet and destroy our enemies forever!

We are the mighty C'Haaf-shaar! DEATH OR GLORY!'

'The mighty C'Haaf-shaar!' yelled the soldiers. 'DEATH OR GLORY!'

'You know, I'm getting *so* bored with hearing that,' muttered Yasmin.

'Excuse me, General,' said Yuri, raising his hand as though he were in class. 'I'd like to be absolutely clear on this. What happens if we refuse to do it?'

'Then we will slaughter all three of you,' squeaked the General, staring at them with his yellow reptilian eyes. 'And destroy your home ship as well.'

'Oh, right, thanks,' said Yuri. 'I had a feeling that's what you might say.'

Five minutes later, the three friends were sitting glumly in their fighter again. Outside Luke could see C'Haaf-shaar fighters taking off, their fleet beginning to gather for the attack on the P'Tush-faar's planet. The General was climbing into his ship too, and gestured angrily at Luke as if to say, *Get on with it, human!*

'Well, that didn't go quite as I planned,' said Luke when they were in space. He checked the rear-view screen – the C'Haaf-shaar fleet was close behind.

'OK,' said Yasmin. 'What's your plan now, Amazing-Super-Space-Combat-Pilot-Luke-Riley? Assuming of course that you do actually *have* a plan?'

'I do, as it happens,' said Luke. 'I'm sorry I didn't listen before, Yasmin. You were dead right. We should just get away from here and head for the *Buzz*.'

'But what about the mega-bomb?' said Yasmin. 'Suppose it goes off? And that big lizard said he'd destroy us and the *Buzz Aldrin* if we tried to escape.'

'Simple,' said Luke, shrugging. 'We'll dump the bomb and radio ahead to my mum. If we give her enough warning, the *Buzz* can be ready to make a run for deep space as soon as we arrive. Can you work out how to do all that, Yuri?

'No problem!' said Yuri, already tapping away furiously at his keyboard.

'Great!' said Luke. He checked the view-screens once more and gripped the joystick tightly. 'Time we showed these aliens a clean pair of exhaust tubes.'

He hit the main thrusters and the fighter shot off, speeding away from the C'Haaf-shaar fleet. The General wasn't slow to react, though. The fleet chased after the fighter, each ship firing its laser cannons. Luke had to use every bit of his skill to dodge through a crazy, glittering neon web of hot, deadly beams.

Suddenly Admiral K'Klem-Tek appeared on the screen in front of him.

'You have betrayed us, Luke Riley,' the Admiral squeaked. 'Prepare to be destroyed!'

'I'd been hoping they'd gone home,' muttered Luke, his heart sinking as he saw that the P'Tush-faar fleet was blocking their way out of the star system.

'They're firing missiles at us, Luke!' said Yuri. 'Impact in seconds!'

'Oh, terrific!' said Yasmin. 'We're really dead this time.'

'I don't think so...' said Luke, eyes fixed on his viewscreens. He'd just remembered the map of the star system Mum had shown him, and it had given him an idea. It was definitely their last chance, and a pretty slim one at that – but it was a chance. 'Plot us a course for the third planet, Yuri. We're going to swing round behind it and shake off both fleets!'

CHAPTER EIGHT
SOMEONE SCARY

Luke's idea seemed to be working. Soon they were heading for the third planet, and most of the missiles whizzed past harmlessly. But one stuck with them, getting closer and closer, and nothing Luke could do shook it off. Suddenly there was a terrific BANG! and the fighter lurched off course. 'Oh no, we've been hit!' Luke yelled, wrestling with the joystick, trying to keep control.

'I don't think we can make it round the planet!' said Yuri, tapping away at his keyboard, an edge of panic in his voice. 'You'll just have to land on it instead!'

'I'd already worked that out for myself!' muttered Luke. 'OK, here we go...'

They plunged into the planet's atmosphere, and within seconds the whole front of the fighter was glowing a hot, deep red. 'Nice colour,' said Yasmin. 'But doesn't it mean we're coming in too steeply and that we're burning up?'

'Hey, I'm very impressed, Yasmin!' said Yuri, looking at her with genuine surprise. 'That's almost geeky! I didn't think you were interested in science.'

'I'm not, usually,' said Yasmin. 'I suppose it's got something to do with the prospect of being burnt to a crisp. Any chance of preventing that, Luke?'

'There might be,' said Luke, gritting his teeth as he pulled on the joystick. 'If you two would just shut up for a minute and let me concentrate, that is...'

The surface of the planet was rushing up towards them and Luke thought it was hopeless, that they would burn up or crash. But just at the last moment he managed to bring the fighter out of its dive, and they skimmed a metre or two above a rocky plain. Luke finally brought them down and they skidded to a halt.

'Phew, what a ride that was!' said Yuri,

laughing. 'Well done, Luke!'

'Yeah, pretty cool, Riley,' agreed Yasmin. 'I take it all back.'

'I'm just glad we're still alive,' said Luke, and glanced out of the cockpit. 'But we're not safe yet. It looks like they're not going to leave us alone...'

Two alien spaceships were coming in to land on either side of them, and the moment they settled their doors flew open. The Admiral stepped out of one with half a dozen of his soldiers close behind him, and the General emerged from the other, also with his personal bodyguard. Both groups headed for the fighter.

'OK, now they're *seriously* starting to irritate me,' muttered Yasmin.

'They've spotted each other,' said Yuri. 'This could be interesting.'

Luke expected total mayhem, of course...

but there was no shooting. There was plenty of *shouting*, though, the General and the Admiral yelling, their faces almost touching, their soldiers joining in. Being inside the fighter meant the children couldn't hear what they were saying, but that only made it funnier. Luke thought it was like watching one of those old silent comedy movies.

'Huh, look at them!' snorted Yasmin. 'They're like badly behaved kids!'

'They don't *know* why they're fighting any more,' said Yuri. 'They don't have a reason except they've always done it. What they need is someone who could make them realise that, so they stop arguing and start behaving sensibly, like us.'

'Someone very scary,' murmured Luke, turning to his friends. 'Have you contacted the *Buzz* yet, Yuri? I think this could well be a job for my mum.'

'Oh yes,' said Yasmin, nodding eagerly. 'I can't think of anyone better.'

Yuri managed to contact Captain Riley, and half an hour later Luke saw the shuttle from the *Buzz Aldrin* coming in to land. His mum emerged from the little craft and the three friends got out of the fighter to go and meet her. The aliens were still yelling and shouting at each other, and took no notice of them.

'Thank goodness you're all right!' Mum said, hugging Luke and smiling at Yuri and Yasmin. 'We've been so worried! What did those aliens do to you?'

'It's a long story,' said Luke, and told her everything that had happened. Mum listened quietly, frowning at first, eventually looking very cross indeed.

'I think *I'll* be the one who tells *them* what's acceptable and what isn't,' she said at last. 'You three stay here while I go and have a word.'

She rolled up the sleeves of her spacesuit and strode over to the arguing aliens. 'QUIET!' the three friends heard her yell, and the aliens instantly fell silent, a couple of the soldiers dropping their lasers, the General and the Admiral looking startled.

Within minutes they were both apologising like mad. Shortly after that, they had agreed to a ceasefire and were setting up a peace committee. Luke suspected they would have agreed to anything, just to stop Mum shouting at them.

'There you go,' he said. 'Mission accomplished, thanks to my mum!'

'But what if they start fighting again once your mum leaves?' said Yuri.

'Ah, I've already thought of that,' said Luke, grinning. 'I'll ask her if we can stay with them for a few days – and teach them how to play computer games!'

'Good thinking!' said Yasmin. 'That ought to keep them out of mischief.'

'Well, it works for us!' said Luke. 'Most of the time, anyway...'